Dragon Clash!

Tony Bradman • Jon Stuart

Contents

OXFORD
UNIVERSITY PRESS

Macro Marvel
(billionaire inventor)

Welcome to Micro World!

Macro Marvel invented Micro World – a micro-sized theme park where you have to shrink to get in.

A computer called **CODE** controls Micro World and all the robots inside – MITEs and BITEs.

A MITE

A BITE

Disaster strikes!

CODE goes wrong on opening day.
CODE wants to shrink the world.

Macro Marvel is trapped inside the park …

Enter Team X!

Four micro agents – *Max, Cat, Ant* and *Tiger* – are sent to rescue Macro Marvel and defeat CODE.

Mini Marvel joins Team X.

Mini Marvel
(Macro's daughter)

Together they have to:

* Defeat the BITEs
* Collect the CODE keys
* Rescue Macro Marvel
* Stop CODE!
* Save the world!

**CODE key
(2 collected)**

Look at the map on page 4. You are in the Dragon Quest zone.

3

Before you read

Sound checker
Say the sounds.

wh   ed

Sound spotter
Blend the sounds.

wh	i	ch

wh	i	zz	ed

y	e	ll	ed

j	u	m	p	ed

Tricky words
said
like

Into the zone
What do you think the
Dragon Quest zone will be like?

5

Jump in the Jeeps

Team X and Mini went into the Dragon Quest zone.

"Wow! This looks good!"
said Tiger.
"I am a big fan of dragons."

Tiger pointed to a big dragon.
"I like that dragon best,"
he said. "Look at its wings!"

"I like the jeeps. They are cool!" said Cat. "Which jeep shall we go in?"

Cat and Tiger jumped into a green jeep and they whizzed off. "Look for the CODE key when you stop!" yelled Mini.

Now you have read ...
Jump in the Jeeps

Text checker
Read the captions and match them to the pictures.

| They whizzed off. | Tiger pointed. | Mini yelled. |

MITE fun
What did Mini yell to Cat and Tiger?
Why do you think she said that?

Before you read

Sound checker

Say the sounds.

wh   ed

Sound spotter

Blend the sounds.

wh	oo	sh	ed

h	i	ss	ed

r	u	sh	ed

f	igh	t

Tricky words

what
said

Into the zone

What might stop Tiger looking for the CODE key?

Tiger and the Dragon

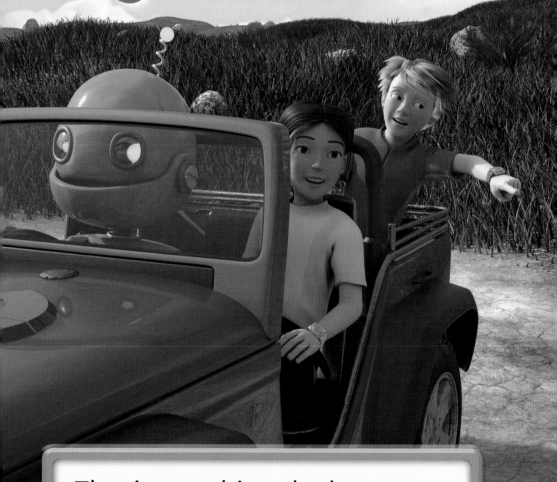

The jeep whizzed along.
"Stop the jeep!" yelled Tiger.
"What is it?" asked Cat.

"Look at that! We can fight dragons!" said Tiger. "I want to join in."

"When will we look for the CODE key?" asked Cat.
"Soon," said Tiger.

Tiger rushed off to fight the dragon.

"I will be the winner!" he yelled.

The dragon hissed and growled at Tiger.
"Help me, Cat!" Tiger howled.
Cat got out her Bee-machine and shrank.

Cat whooshed up to the dragon.
"Look at me, dragon!" she said.

The dragon turned to look at Cat.
Tiger ran with all his might.

"I will win next time!" said Tiger. Just then, an even bigger dragon appeared.

"What is that?" asked Tiger. "It is the BITE! We need a good plan to fight that one," said Cat.

Now you have read ...
Tiger and the Dragon

Text checker

Read the words and then
find them in the story.
Read the text again.

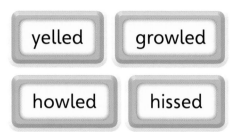

yelled   growled

howled   hissed

MITE fun

Look back at the story.
How did Tiger feel ...

... before the dragon fight?   ... after the dragon fight?

Look out for me!

24